THE STORY OF THE
TENNESSEE TITANS

WARREN MOON, EARL CAMPBELL, LORENZO WHITE, ERNEST GIVINS, CHARLEY HENNIGAN, FRANK WYCHECK, LEON GRAY, BRAD HOPKINS, BRUCE MATTHEWS, MIKE MUNCHAK, CARL MAUCK, ELVIN BETHEA, JEVON KEARSE, CURLEY CULP, RAY CHILDRESS, ROBERT BRAZILE, AL SMITH, CRIS DISHMAN, WILLIE ALEXANDER, GEORGE WEBSTER, KEN HOUSTON, JIM NORTON, AL DEL GRECO, GREG MONTGOMERY, WARREN MOON, EARL CAMPBELL, LORENZO WHITE, ERNEST GIVINS, CHARLEY HENNIGAN, FRANK WYCHECK, LEON GRAY, BRAD HOPKINS

THE STORY OF THE TENNESSEE TITANS

BY JIM WHITING

CREATIVE EDUCATION / CREATIVE PAPERBACKS

PUBLISHED BY CREATIVE EDUCATION AND CREATIVE PAPERBACKS
P.O. BOX 227, MANKATO, MINNESOTA 56002
CREATIVE EDUCATION AND CREATIVE PAPERBACKS ARE IMPRINTS OF THE
CREATIVE COMPANY
WWW.THECREATIVECOMPANY.US

DESIGN AND PRODUCTION BY BLUE DESIGN (WWW.BLUEDES.COM)
ART DIRECTION BY RITA MARSHALL
PRINTED IN CHINA

PHOTOGRAPHS BY AP IMAGES (ASSOCIATED PRESS), GETTY IMAGES (BRIAN
BAHR, FREDERICK BREEDON, JONATHAN DANIEL/ALLSPORT, STEPHEN DUNN,
FOCUS ON SPORT, SAM GREENWOOD, GRANT HALVERSON, ALLEN KEE/NFL,
NEIL LEIFER/SI, ANDY LYONS, AL MESSERSCHMIDT, AL MESSERSCHMIDT/NFL,
RONALD C. MODRA/SPORTS IMAGERY, JOSEPH PATRONITE, DOUG PENSINGER,
PAUL SPINELLI, MATTHEW STOCKMAN, GEORGE TIEDEMANN/SI, LOU WITT/NFL,
MICHAEL ZAGARIS), NEWSCOM (ROBIN ALAM/ICON SPORTSWIRE 164, SAM
JORDAN/SPORTSCHROME, MIKE STRASINGER/ADMEDIA, WILLIAM PURNELL/ICON
SPORTSWIRE CBG, SCOTT WINTERS/ICON SPORTSWIRE DGM)

NAMES: WHITING, JIM, AUTHOR.
TITLE: THE STORY OF THE TENNESSEE TITANS / JIM WHITING.
SERIES: NFL TODAY.
INCLUDES INDEX.
SUMMARY: THIS HIGH-INTEREST HISTORY OF THE NATIONAL FOOTBALL
LEAGUE'S TENNESSEE TITANS HIGHLIGHTS MEMORABLE GAMES, SUMMARIZES
SEASONAL TRIUMPHS AND DEFEATS, AND FEATURES STANDOUT PLAYERS SUCH
AS MARCUS MARIOTA.
IDENTIFIERS: LCCN 2018060967 / ISBN 978-1-64026-160-0 (HARDCOVER) / ISBN
978-1-62832-723-6 (PBK) / ISBN 978-1-64000-278-4 (EBOOK)
SUBJECTS: LCSH: TENNESSEE TITANS (FOOTBALL TEAM)—HISTORY—JUVENILE
LITERATURE.
CLASSIFICATION: LCC GV956.T45 W55 2019 / DDC 796.332/640976855—DC23

FIRST EDITION HC 9 8 7 6 5 4 3 2 1
FIRST EDITION PBK 9 8 7 6 5 4 3 2 1

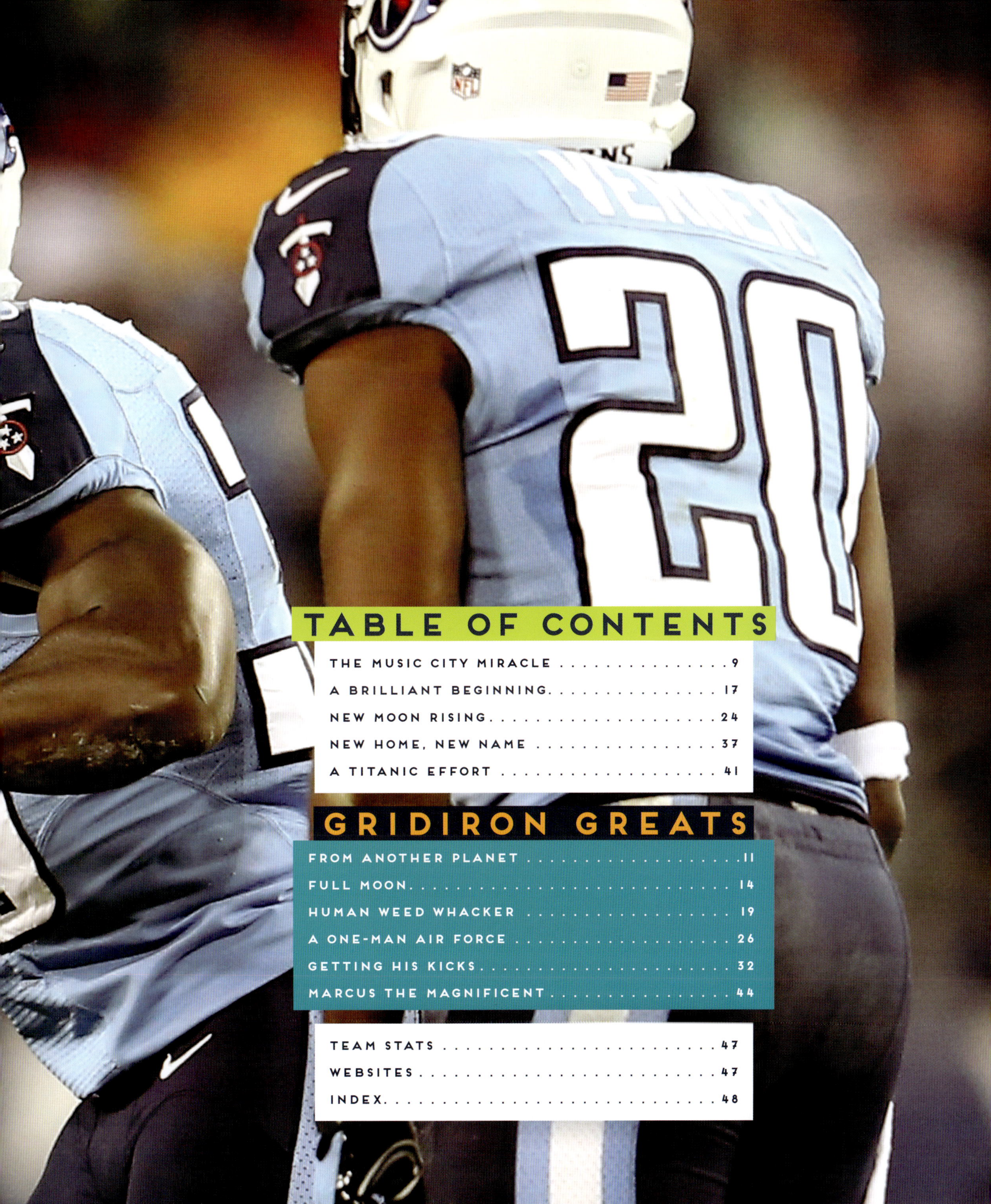

TABLE OF CONTENTS

GRIDIRON GREATS

THE MUSIC CITY MIRACLE

One of the most exciting plays in NFL (National Football League) history came near the end of a playoff game in January 2000. The Tennessee Titans hosted the Buffalo Bills at Adelphia Coliseum in Nashville. The Titans led, 12–0, at halftime. The Bills came back to take a 13–12 lead in the fourth quarter. With two minutes left, Tennessee kicked a field goal. The Titans regained the lead. Then Buffalo kicked a field goal with just 16 seconds remaining. The Bills were up, 16–15.

The teams lined up for the kickoff. "Do the Titans have a miracle left in them?" asked the TV announcer. "If they do, they need it now." The Bills decided to do a "pooch" kick. It was higher and shorter than usual. Titans running back Lorenzo Neal received the kick on the 25-yard line. He

spun and handed the ball to tight end Frank Wycheck. Wycheck took several steps to his right. He threw the ball back across the field. Wide receiver Kevin Dyson caught it. He had several blockers in front of him. He raced 75 yards along the sideline. He scored the game-winning touchdown. "It's a miracle!" the announcer screamed. "Tennessee has pulled [off] a miracle!"

Part of the miracle was that Dyson had never practiced the play. He replaced an injured teammate who normally would have been part of the play. In fact, Titans coach Jeff Fisher was still explaining it as Dyson ran onto the field. "It was like being a little kid again, drawing something up in the dirt and then going out and doing it," Wycheck said.

Bills coach Wade Phillips challenged the play. He was sure that Wycheck had thrown the ball forward. That would have been a penalty. The touchdown would not count. At first it seemed that Phillips was right. But the officials eventually agreed that it was a lateral, or sideways pass. Wycheck's arm was beyond the 25-yard line when he released the ball. Dyson caught the ball when it was almost on the line itself. That meant the path of the ball was slightly backward. It was perfectly legal. The touchdown stood. Tennessee won. Nashville is the "capital" of the country music industry. Because of this,

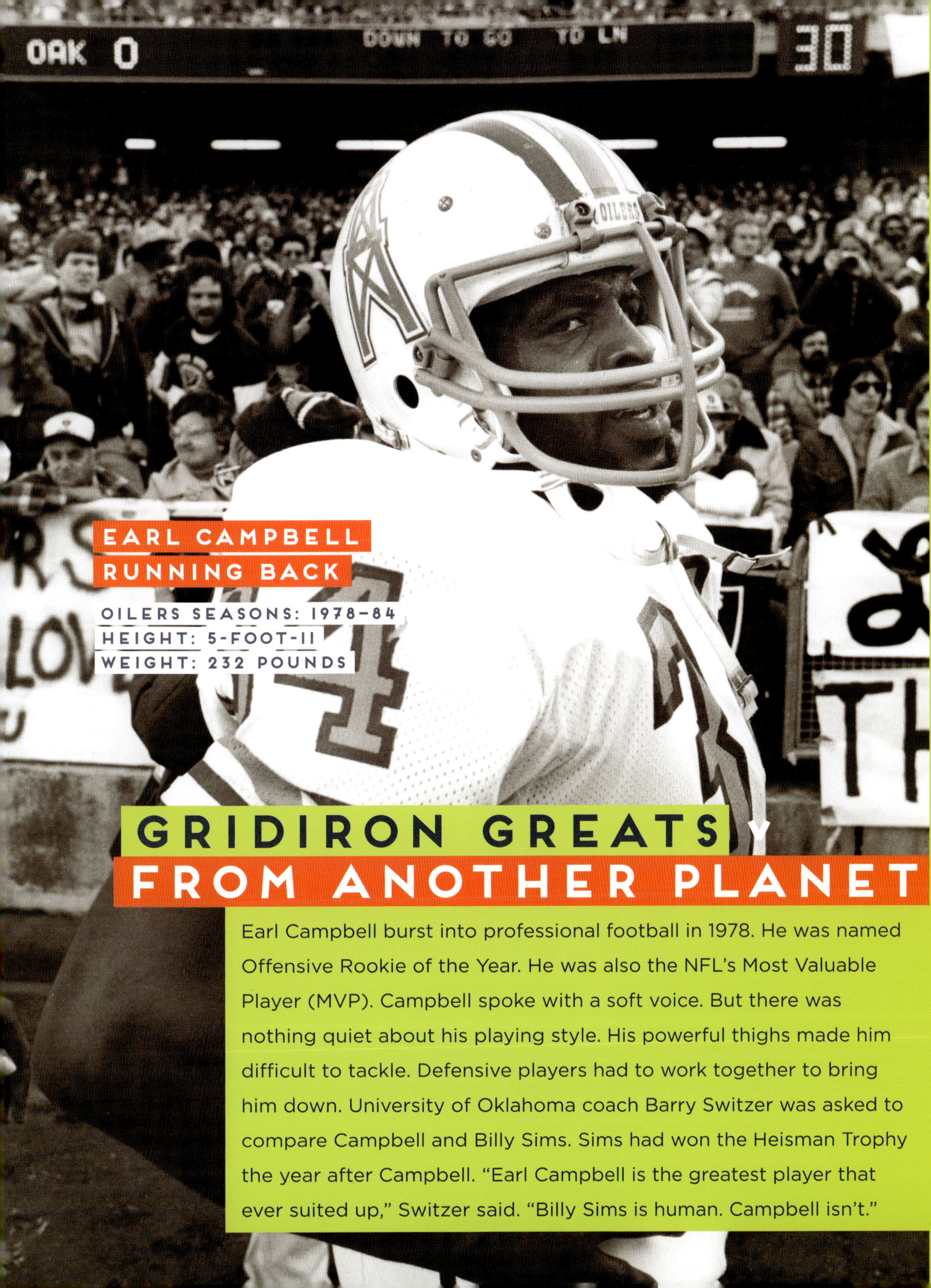

EARL CAMPBELL
RUNNING BACK

OILERS SEASONS: 1978–84
HEIGHT: 5-FOOT-11
WEIGHT: 232 POUNDS

GRIDIRON GREATS FROM ANOTHER PLANET

Earl Campbell burst into professional football in 1978. He was named Offensive Rookie of the Year. He was also the NFL's Most Valuable Player (MVP). Campbell spoke with a soft voice. But there was nothing quiet about his playing style. His powerful thighs made him difficult to tackle. Defensive players had to work together to bring him down. University of Oklahoma coach Barry Switzer was asked to compare Campbell and Billy Sims. Sims had won the Heisman Trophy the year after Campbell. "Earl Campbell is the greatest player that ever suited up," Switzer said. "Billy Sims is human. Campbell isn't."

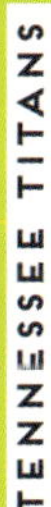

RUNNING BACK EDDIE GEORGE

"IT'S A MIRACLE!" THE ANNOUNCER SCREAMED. "TENNESSEE HAS PULLED [OFF] A MIRACLE."

it is often called "Music City." So the unlikely victory was quickly dubbed the "Music City Miracle."

Titans fans may have felt the outcome was a form of payback. Seven years earlier, the Titans were known as the Houston Oilers. They faced Buffalo in the playoffs. The Oilers had taken a 35–3 lead early in the third quarter. The Houston radio announcer crowed, "The lights are on here at Rich Stadium [Buffalo's home field], but you might as well turn them off … this one is over." He was wrong. Buffalo stormed back. The game was tied at the end of the fourth quarter. The Bills kicked a field goal to win in overtime. It was the biggest comeback in NFL history.

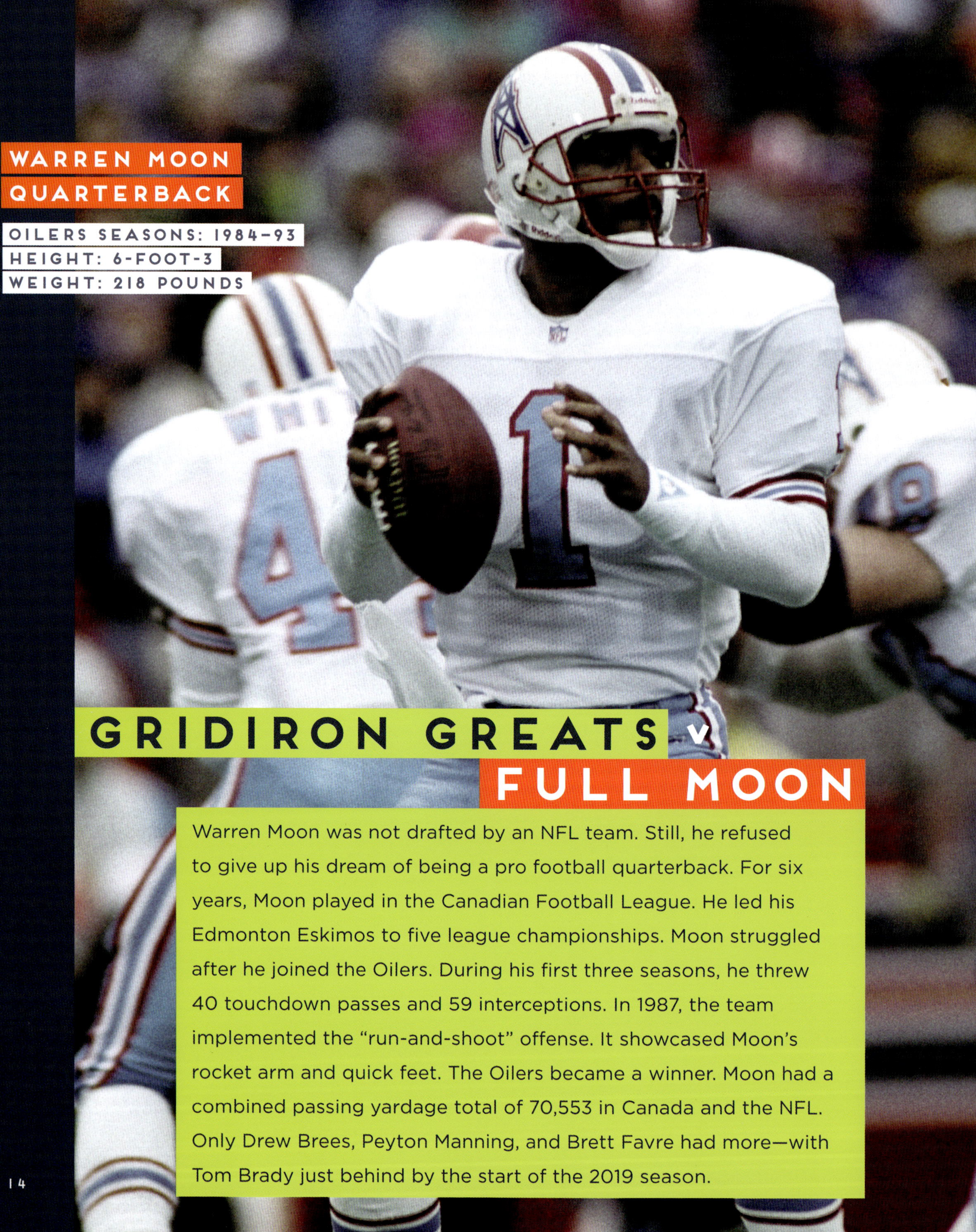

GRIDIRON GREATS v
FULL MOON

Warren Moon was not drafted by an NFL team. Still, he refused to give up his dream of being a pro football quarterback. For six years, Moon played in the Canadian Football League. He led his Edmonton Eskimos to five league championships. Moon struggled after he joined the Oilers. During his first three seasons, he threw 40 touchdown passes and 59 interceptions. In 1987, the team implemented the "run-and-shoot" offense. It showcased Moon's rocket arm and quick feet. The Oilers became a winner. Moon had a combined passing yardage total of 70,553 in Canada and the NFL. Only Drew Brees, Peyton Manning, and Brett Favre had more—with Tom Brady just behind by the start of the 2019 season.

313

208

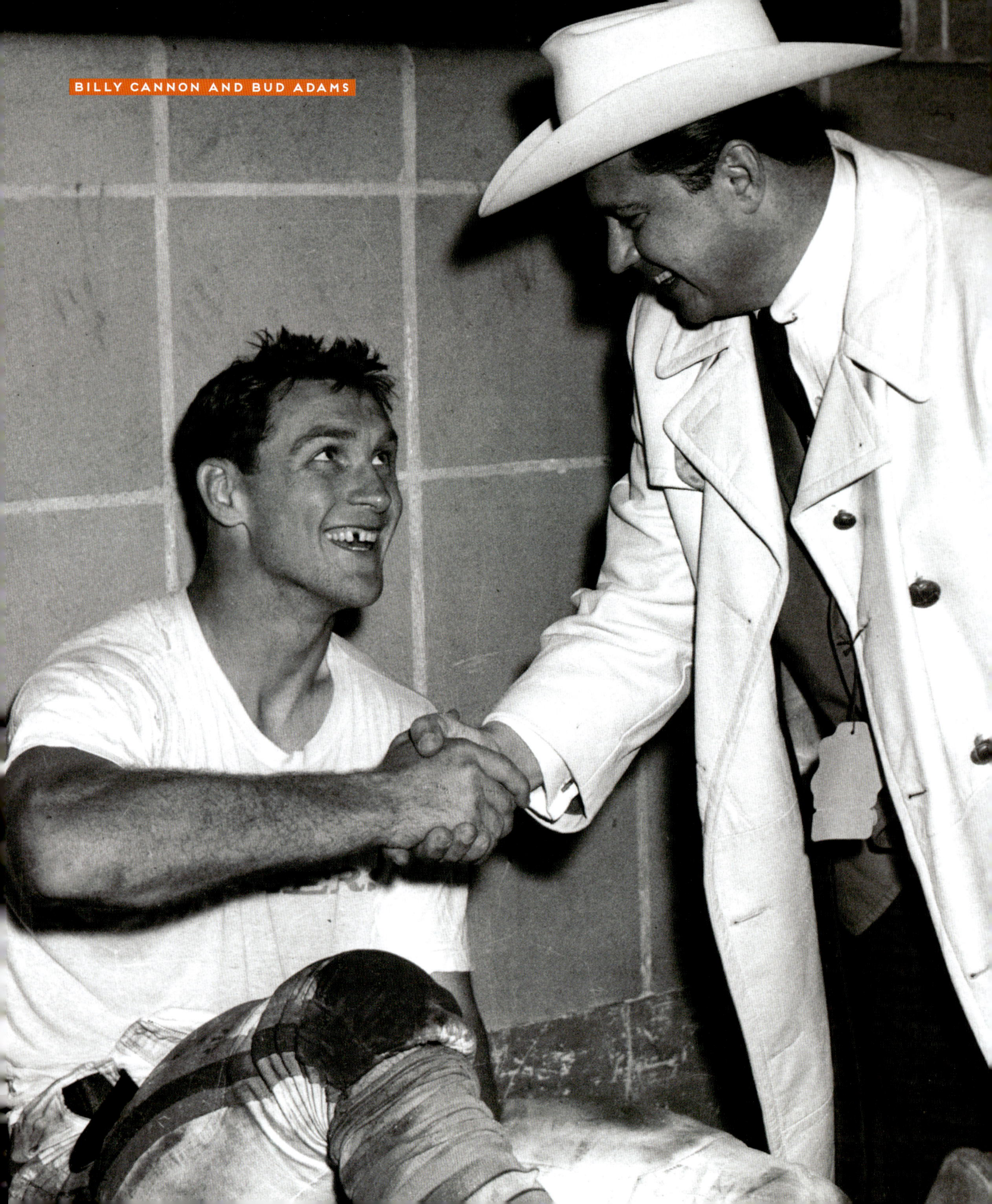
BILLY CANNON AND BUD ADAMS

A BRILLIANT BEGINNING

The Titans began in Texas in 1959. Houston oil company executive K. S. "Bud" Adams joined with seven other millionaires to form the American Football League (AFL). Adams named his team the Oilers. The Oilers enjoyed immediate success. They outbid the Los Angeles Rams of the NFL to sign running back Billy Cannon. He had just won the Heisman Trophy as the best player in college football. This boosted the AFL's credibility as a professional league.

In their first season, the Oilers went 10–4. They won the AFL's Eastern Division. They beat the Los Angeles Chargers in the AFL Championship Game. Later, quarterback George Blanda boasted, "That first year, the Houston Oilers or

14

296

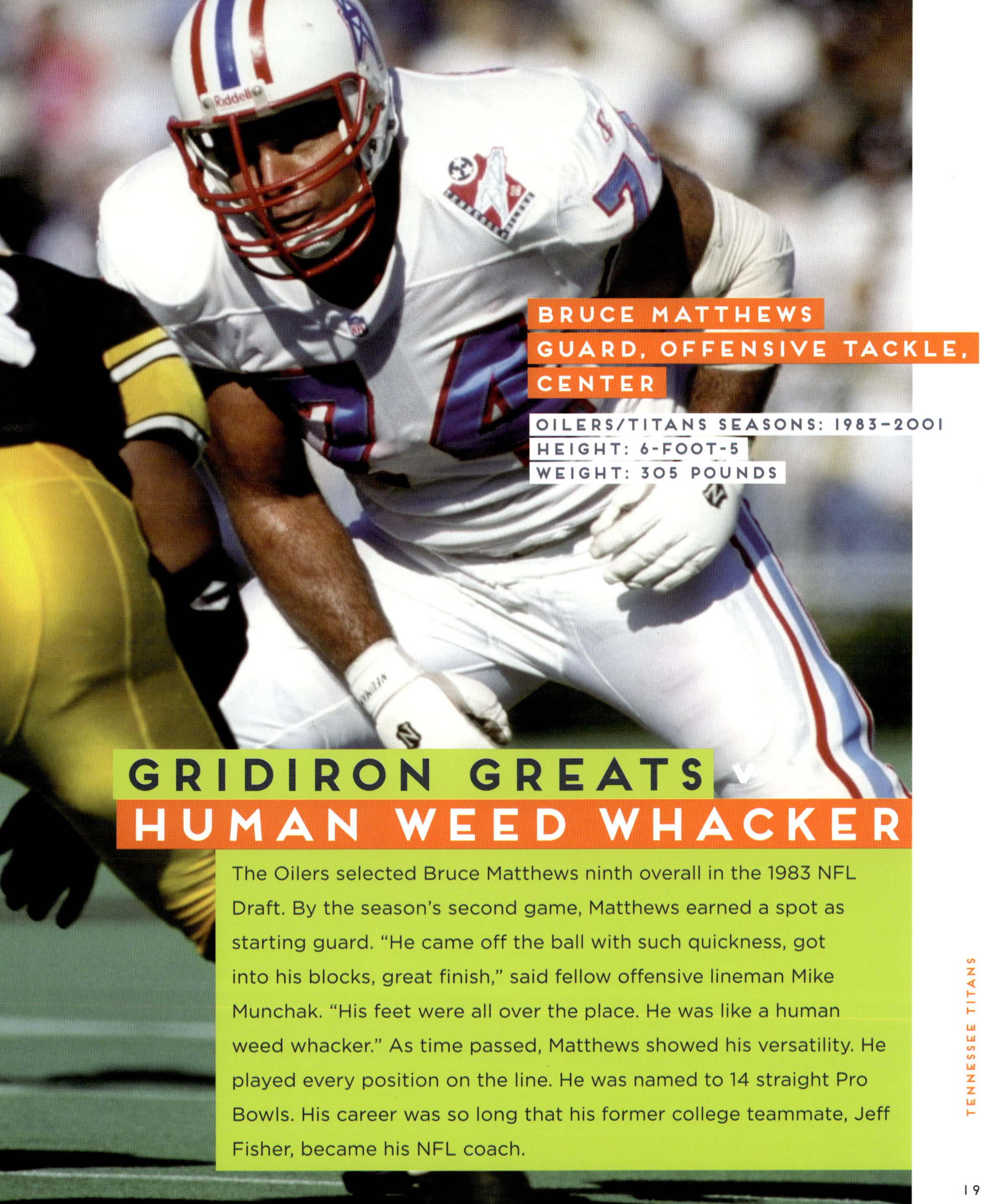

GRIDIRON GREATS
HUMAN WEED WHACKER

The Oilers selected Bruce Matthews ninth overall in the 1983 NFL Draft. By the season's second game, Matthews earned a spot as starting guard. "He came off the ball with such quickness, got into his blocks, great finish," said fellow offensive lineman Mike Munchak. "His feet were all over the place. He was like a human weed whacker." As time passed, Matthews showed his versatility. He played every position on the line. He was named to 14 straight Pro Bowls. His career was so long that his former college teammate, Jeff Fisher, became his NFL coach.

DEFENSIVE END ELVIN BETHEA

the Los Angeles Chargers could have beaten the NFL champion [Philadelphia Eagles] in a Super Bowl."

Cannon led the charge in 1961. He ran for 948 yards. It was the best in the AFL. The Oilers finished the season at 10–3–1. Once again, they played the Chargers for the AFL championship. The Oilers won their second title.

Fans hoped for a "three-peat" in 1962. The Oilers made the championship game again. This time, they faced the Dallas Texans. The game went into double overtime. The Texans beat the Oilers, 20–17. That loss was the start of a disappointing stretch for the Oilers. Age and injuries bogged down the team. Houston finished the next four seasons with losing records. The Oilers climbed back to a 9–4–1 record in 1967. But they lost to the Oakland Raiders in the championship game, 40–7. Two years later, Houston faced the Raiders again in the championship. Oakland overwhelmed them, 56–7.

The AFL and NFL merged in 1970. Afterward, the Oilers struggled. Houston finished 1972 and 1973 with just one win each year. The Oilers named O. A. "Bum" Phillips as head coach in 1975. He looked like a stereotypical Texan. He wore a ten-gallon hat, snakeskin boots, and Western shirts. He lined up his team in a "3-4" defense. It had three linemen with four linebackers behind them. This formation was especially effective at stopping the run.

The Oilers finished with a solid 10–4 record in 1975. The team was hit hard by injuries the next two seasons. It went just 5–9 and 8–6. In 1978, Houston became a powerhouse. The Oilers drafted Earl Campbell. He was

GEORGE BLANDA AND GUARD BOB TALAMINI

"THAT FIRST YEAR, THE HOUSTON OILERS COULD HAVE BEATEN THE NFL CHAMPION [PHILADELPHIA EAGLES] IN A SUPER BOWL."

—GEORGE BLANDA

a bruising 230-pound running back. He was named both Rookie of the Year and Offensive Player of the Year. Fans began to call the Oilers the "Earlers." They beat the Dolphins in the first round of the playoffs. They then sailed past the New England Patriots. They met the Pittsburgh Steelers for the American Football Conference (AFC) Championship Game. Unfortunately, the Oilers committed nine turnovers. They lost, 34–5.

In 1979, the Oilers were back in the AFC Championship Game. It was a rematch with Pittsburgh. Houston lost again. The next year, Oakland bounced Houston from the playoffs. The Oilers fired Phillips. By the early 1980s, most of the Oilers' stars had retired. Others moved to different teams. The Oilers were among the worst teams in the NFL. In 1983, they scraped together just two wins.

EARL CAMPBELL

NEW MOON RISING

In 1984, Houston signed quarterback Warren Moon. He had been a star in the Canadian Football League. He completed his first NFL season with 3,338 passing yards. It was a new team record.

During the 1985 season, defensive coordinator Jerry Glanville was promoted to head coach. Glanville was famous for his black clothes and sharp wit. The Oilers played their home games at the Houston Astrodome. Glanville said he wanted to turn it into a "House of Pain." He thought the team should be more aggressive. "When I came here in '84, we had the nicest guys in the NFL," Glanville said. "But they couldn't hit if you handed them sticks."

GRIDIRON GREATS ᵛ
A ONE-MAN AIR FORCE

Steve McNair was nicknamed "Air" during college. He made big plays with his rifle of an arm. McNair also showed tremendous running skill. He stayed calm under pressure. He led his team to its only Super Bowl appearance. He won league co-MVP honors in 2003. McNair was highly respected in Nashville. He died tragically in 2009. Thousands of people turned out for his funeral. "If ever there was a better connection between a city and a player, I haven't seen it," sportswriter Clay Travis wrote. "McNair and Nashville were a perfect pair."

211

161

Glanville boosted his defense with swift cornerback Cris Dishman. Offensive lineman Bruce Matthews stabilized the offense. Moon was a fan favorite. Crowds flocked to the Astrodome. The Oilers did not disappoint them. Houston finished 9–6 in 1987. It made the playoffs that year. The team appeared in the playoffs every year for the next six years.

But the Oilers always fell short of the Super Bowl. In 1990, former linebacker Jack Pardee replaced Glanville. Pardee wanted to take advantage of Moon's strong arm and scrambling ability. The coach installed the "run-

ERNEST GIVINS

and-shoot" offense. It used four wide receivers and no tight end. Moon thrived. He fired passes to the talented receiving trio of Drew Hill, Ernest Givins, and Haywood Jeffires. In a December 1990 game, he passed for 527 yards. In 1990 and 1991, Moon threw for nearly 4,700 yards each season. In 1991, Jeffires and Hill together caught 190 receptions. It was the most by two teammates in one season.

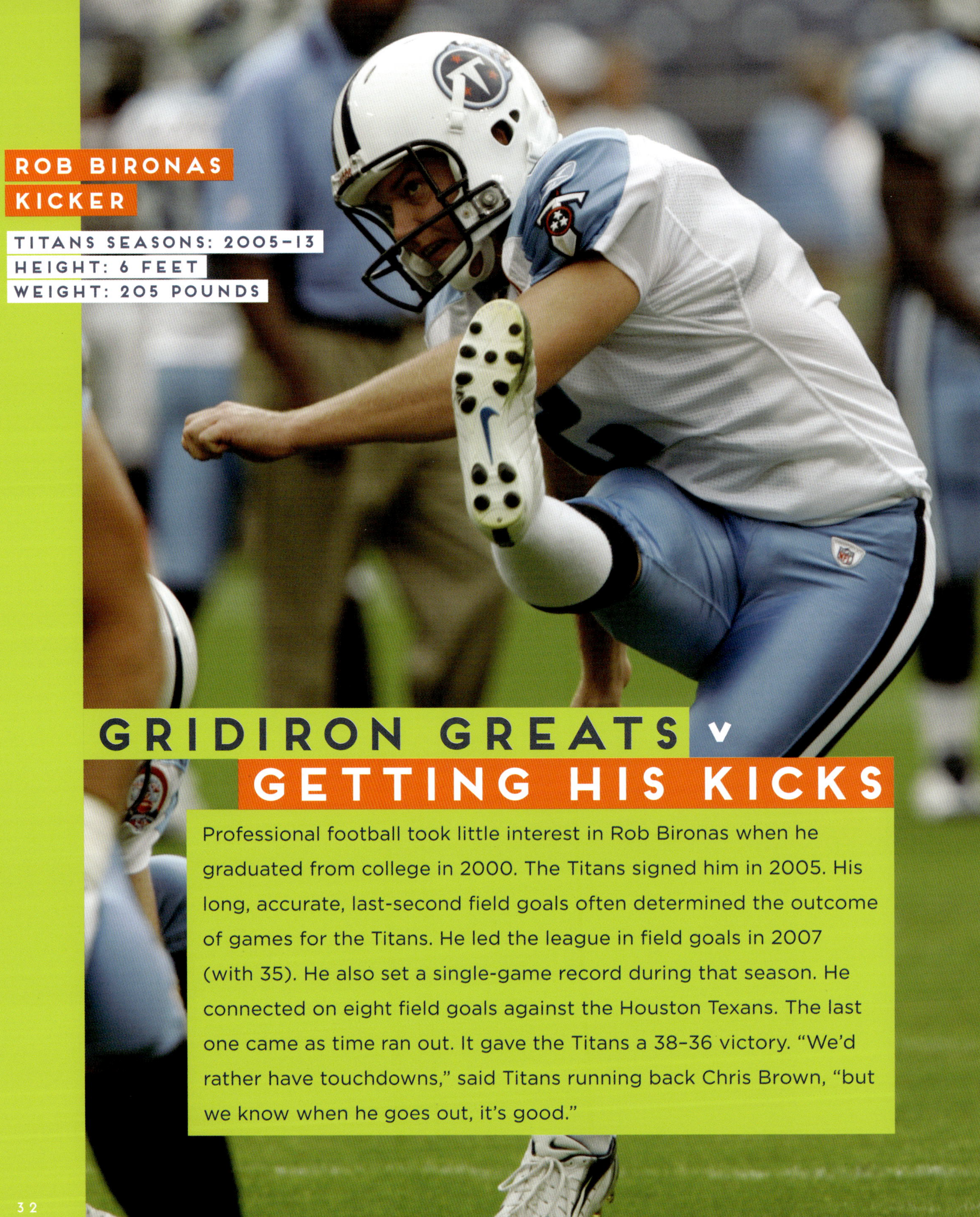

GRIDIRON GREATS ᵛ
GETTING HIS KICKS

Professional football took little interest in Rob Bironas when he graduated from college in 2000. The Titans signed him in 2005. His long, accurate, last-second field goals often determined the outcome of games for the Titans. He led the league in field goals in 2007 (with 35). He also set a single-game record during that season. He connected on eight field goals against the Houston Texans. The last one came as time ran out. It gave the Titans a 38–36 victory. "We'd rather have touchdowns," said Titans running back Chris Brown, "but we know when he goes out, it's good."

239

144

In 1993, the Oilers finished 12–4. The following year, they traded Moon to the Minnesota Vikings. Fans were disappointed. Without Moon, the Oilers plummeted to 2–14. It was the largest single-season drop in wins in NFL history. Pardee was fired. Defensive coordinator Jeff Fisher became head coach. He rebuilt the roster. Houston drafted quarterback Steve "Air" McNair in 1995. McNair could launch long bombs. He could scramble for a first down, too. The next year, the team added running back Eddie George. He earned NFL Offensive Rookie of the Year honors. He was a bruising, durable runner. He never missed a game because of injury.

JEVON KEARSE

NEW HOME, NEW NAME

In addition to roster changes, the Oilers made a location change. Adams wanted a new stadium for his team. But Houston civic officials gave him little support. So he moved the Oilers to Tennessee in 1997. The first year, the Oilers played in Memphis. They moved to Vanderbilt Stadium in Nashville for the next season. The Oilers went 8–8 both times. Meanwhile, fans clamored for a name that better suited the team's new home. Nashville was known as the "Athens of the South." Adams took a name from Greek mythology: Titans.

The Titans also had a new star. He was rookie defensive end Jevon Kearse. He had rare speed and agility. His nickname was "The Freak." The Titans

finished 13–3. It was the best record in team history. Tennessee rolled through the playoffs. First came the Music City Miracle. Then the Titans knocked off the Indianapolis Colts and Jacksonville Jaguars. They reached the Super Bowl. They faced the high-scoring St. Louis Rams. In the third quarter, the Rams led, 16–0. Tennessee came back to tie the game. With less than two minutes left, the Rams took a 23–16 lead. McNair drove the Titans down the field. But receiver Kevin Dyson was pulled down one yard short of the end zone. The game was over.

After that, the Titans remained one of the top teams in the NFL. Tennessee made the playoffs in 2000, 2002, and 2003. The team posted records of 13–3, 11–5, and 12–4 during those years. But the 2003 season signaled the end of an era in Tennessee. The Titans released George. Two years later, they traded McNair. They had selected quarterback Vince Young with the third overall pick in the 2006 NFL Draft.

At 6-foot-5, Young was a bigger version of McNair. The rookie wasted no time. He showed a knack for leading his team to comeback victories. In November 2006, the Titans faced the New York Giants. After three quarters, the Giants led, 21–0. Young led the biggest fourth-quarter rally in the club's history. He threw a four-yard touchdown pass. He ran the ball for a score. Then he tossed another touchdown with less than a minute left on the clock. The Titans defense made an interception. In the final seconds, kicker Rob Bironas nailed a 49-yard field goal. The Titans won. Young was named to the Pro Bowl. He was the first rookie quarterback in more than 20 years to receive the honor.

In 2007, the Titans fought their way to a 10–6 record. It was good enough for a playoff spot. But the San Diego Chargers beat them, 17–6.

A TITANIC EFFORT

Tennessee was one of the biggest stories in the NFL in 2008. It started the season 10–0 and finished 13–3. Rookie running back Chris Johnson ran for more than 1,200 yards. The Titans faced the Baltimore Ravens in the playoffs. Unfortunately, the Titans turned the ball over three times and lost. That ended an otherwise superb season on a sour note.

The 2009 season was disappointing. The Titans started at 0–6. They endured an embarrassing loss. The Patriots demolished them, 59–0. The Titans won their next five games. They ended the season at

8–8. Along the way, Johnson rushed for 2,006 yards. He became only the sixth player in NFL history to reach the 2,000-yard mark in a season. But that effort was not good enough for the playoffs.

The 2010 season started much better. The Titans won five of their first seven games. But they finished with a disappointing 6–10 record. Fisher was fired. Mike Munchak was brought in as the new head coach. He had been an offensive lineman for the Oilers. He had been selected to the Pro Bowl nine times during his career.

In 2011, Tennessee drafted Jake Locker in the first round. The Titans hoped to build a strong offense around the young quarterback. The team put together a 9–7 record in 2011. But Locker suffered a series of injuries. The Titans endured losing seasons for the next four years. In 2015, the Titans drafted quarterback Marcus Mariota. He set several NFL rookie passing records. The Titans won just three games. But Mariota gave them hope for the future. With a year of experience behind him, Mariota helped Tennessee go 9–7 in 2016. The team narrowly missed the playoffs.

The Titans went 9–7 again in 2017. This time, it was good enough for the playoffs. They met the Kansas City Chiefs in the first round. At halftime, the Titans trailed the Chiefs, 21–3. But early in the third quarter, Mariota rifled the ball toward the end zone. A Chiefs defender

JAKE LOCKER

Marcus Mariota grew up in Hawaii. He did not play football during his first years in high school. Before his senior year, he attended a University of Oregon football camp. The coaches were impressed. They offered him a scholarship. That decision paid off. Mariota was the Pac-12 Conference Offensive Freshman of the Year in 2012. Two years later, he won the Heisman Trophy. Then he entered the 2015 NFL Draft. The Titans took him with the second overall choice. He passed for nearly 3,000 yards and 19 touchdowns as a rookie. Early in the 2018 season, he passed the 10,000 mark in total passing yardage.

MARCUS MARIOTA
QUARTERBACK
TITANS SEASONS: 2015–PRESENT
HEIGHT: 6-FOOT-4
WEIGHT: 222 POUNDS
TENNESSEE TITANS
45

deflected the ball. It went right to Mariota. He caught it and tumbled into the end zone. That made him the first player in NFL playoff history to throw a touchdown pass to himself. The play sparked Tennessee to a 22–21 victory. But Tennessee fell to New England the following week. In 2018, the team repeated its 9–7 record. This time, it wasn't good enough for the postseason.

The Tennessee Titans have never enjoyed a Super Bowl victory. But a winning tradition has been part of the franchise throughout much of its history. Tennessee fans are confident that their Titans will soon bring the Lombardi trophy home to Nashville.

AFL CHAMPIONSHIPS

1960, 1961

WEBSITES

TENNESSEE TITANS

https://www.titansonline.com

NFL: TENNESSEE TITANS TEAM PAGE

http://www.nfl.com/teams/tennesseetitans/profile?team=TEN

INDEX